PUFFIN BOOKS

CATS, DOGS AND CROCODILES

Daniel Postgate lives in Whitstable, Kent. He has worked as a newspaper cartoonist for many years and more recently has written and illustrated a number of children's books. He likes swimming, walking, cooking and watching the telly.

Daniel Postgate

Cats, Dogs and Crocodiles

PUFFIN BOOKS

PUFFIN BOOKS

Published by the Penguin Group
Penguin Books Ltd, 80 Strand, London WC2R 0RL, England
Penguin Putnam Inc., 375 Hudson Street, New York, New York 10014, USA
Penguin Books Australia Ltd, Ringwood, Victoria, Australia
Penguin Books Canada Ltd, 10 Alcorn Avenue, Toronto, Ontario, Canada M4V 3B2
Penguin Books India (P) Ltd, 11 Community Centre, Panchsheel Park, New Dehli – 110 0117, India
Penguin Books (NZ) Ltd, Cnr Rosedale and Airborne Roads, Albany, Auckland, New Zealand
Penguin Books (South Africa) (Pty) 24 Sturdee Avenue, Rosebank 2196, South Africa

Penguin Books Ltd, Registered Offices: 80 Strand, London WC2R 0RL, England

www.penguin.com

First published 2001
3 5 7 9 10 8 6 4 2

Copyright © Daniel Postgate, 2001
All rights reserved

The moral right of the author and illustrator has been asserted

Set in Bembo

Printed in Hong Kong by Midas Printing Ltd

British Library Cataloguing in Publication Data
A CIP catalogue record for this book is available from the British Library

ISBN 0–141–30917–2

"All right then, you win, if it has to be
done ...
I'll buy you a pet. But *one* pet, just one."

1

"Oh thanks, Mum,
so let's get a nice
fluffy cat."

"No no, not a cat.
No, I'm not having
that.
It's a dog that we
want."

2

"No it's not, it's a cat."

"It's a dog."

"It's a cat."

"IT'S A DOG."

"IT'S A CAT."

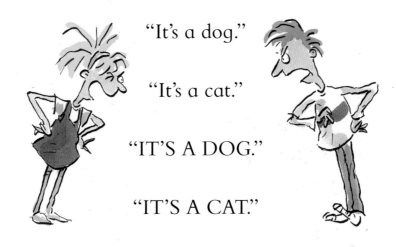

"DON'T SQUABBLE!
I know, put them both to the test,
then *I* will decide on which pet is the best."

"Oh come along, Mum,
you're not in two minds.
You know dogs are best and
there's so many kinds:

there are big ones

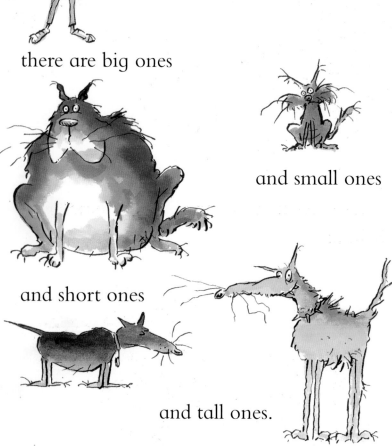

and small ones

and short ones

and tall ones.

4

And ones that are kind,
like the dogs for the blind."

"And ones that are nasty and bite your behind!

No, cats are the best; and just look at the choice:

you've got tabby and ginger and even tortoise.

You've got black ones and brown ones,

thin ones and round ones.

And ones that are snuggly and sleep on your bed."

"And others that fall out of trees on your head!

No, dogs are the best, you can teach
them great tricks:
they'll roll on their backs
and they'll chase
after sticks."

"Well, cats can play games and that sort
of thing.

If there's one
thing they love
it's a
sock
on a string.

And they also
climb trees -"

"Yes, but then I have found
that a fireman is needed
to get them back down.

Now dogs are so handy, they bark and
they bite.
And scare away robbers who creep in at
night."

"But think what will happen when
friends come around.
They're also scared off by a
snap-happy hound.

What we want is a cat
who can chase away mice,
and other such creatures
        that aren't very
            nice."

"But *I've* never seen any cat doing that!
All cats do all day is snooze and cat-nap.

While a dog is a chum you can take to
the park for a hoot and a giggle,
a chuckle, a lark.

They're up for all sorts of great fun and
high jinks –"

"Like rolling in something quite horrid that stinks!

And then try to wash them, that's not such a laugh.

Quite often it's *you* who ends up in the bath.

Now a dog and a door – that's a game
you can't win.
They howl to go out, then they yowl to
come in.

You're a slave to that dopey old hound's
beck and call.
With a cat and a
flap there's no
trouble at all.

They can let themselves in with a
flipperty-flap!"

"And so can their friends for a
snickerty-snack!

But those chums aren't so bad, they're a
generous bunch,
and are far too polite to expect a free
lunch.

So they leave something special for
ankles and knees:
it's a gift you can treasure for ever –

their FLEAS!"

"Here's some advice when it's dinner
time, mate,
don't let your eyes stray away from your
plate.

It just takes a moment, when you are not
looking,

for dogs to scoff down your mum's
home-made cooking.

And here is a tip - when you've grabbed
the best spot,
the cosiest, comfiest chair of the lot,

don't get up and leave it, no not for a
minute

because you'll return to find somebody in it."

"Well, take it from me, it's the cat you can thank
when you no longer find any fish in your tank.

And the cat is to blame when you fling
back the sheets
and find a dead mouse that's
been rotting
for weeks.

So you see
cats are worse."

"No no no, it is dogs."

"Cats."

"Dogs, dogs."

"Cats, cats."

"DOGS."

"CATS."

"DOGS!"

"CATS,

CATS,

CATS!"

"OK, OK! Enough is enough,
I've heard quite enough of this cat and
dog stuff.

To choose either beast you would have to
be mad,

so I'll leave the choice
up to your dear dotty
dad."

"To tell you the truth,"
said their dad with a smile,
"I've always quite fancied
a pet *crocodile*."

Mum thanked her dear husband for being so wise

then nipped down to the pet shop to buy their surprise.

And when she returned, just imagine
their glee
at the sight of not one pet,
not two pets,
but three!

"Here are the creatures you wanted
so badly.
I even bought one for your silly old
daddy."

"Oh thank you, dear Mum!" they
both cried in one voice.

Though I'm not sure if Dad was so
pleased with his choice.